Rooster Combs

Kelly Doudna

Illustrated by Anne Haberstroh

Consulting Editor, Diane Craig, M.A./Reading Specialist

Published by ABDO Publishing Company, 4940 Viking Drive, Edina, Minnesota 55435.

Printed in the United States.

Credits
Edited by: Pam Price
Curriculum Coordinator: Nancy Tuminelly
Cover and Interior Design and Production: Mighty Media
Photo Credits: Brand X Pictures, Digital Vision, John Foxx, Photodisc, ShutterStock

Library of Congress Cataloging-in-Publication Data

Doudna, Kelly, 1963-
    Rooster combs / Kelly Doudna ; illustrated by Anne Haberstroh.
       p. cm. -- (Fact & fiction. Animal tales)
    Summary: Rex is not a morning chicken, so he asks his wife to take over his job of crowing at dawn and opens a beauty salon, where he specializes in comb styling. Includes facts about chickens.
    ISBN 1-59679-965-X (hardcover)
    ISBN 1-59679-966-8 (paperback)
    [1. Beauty shops--Fiction. 2. Job satisfaction--Fiction. 3. Roosters--Fiction. 4. Chickens--Fiction.]
  I. Haberstroh, Anne, ill. II. Title. III. Series.

    PZ7.D74425Roo 2006
    [E]--dc22

2005027839

SandCastle Level: Fluent

SandCastle™ books are created by a professional team of educators, reading specialists, and content developers around five essential components—phonemic awareness, phonics, vocabulary, text comprehension, and fluency—to assist young readers as they develop reading skills and strategies and increase their general knowledge. All books are written, reviewed, and leveled for guided reading, early reading intervention, and Accelerated Reader® programs for use in shared, guided, and independent reading and writing activities to support a balanced approach to literacy instruction. The SandCastle™ series has four levels that correspond to early literacy development. The levels help teachers and parents select appropriate books for young readers.

Emerging Readers
(no flags)

Beginning Readers
(1 flag)

Transitional Readers
(2 flags)

Fluent Readers
(3 flags)

These levels are meant only as a guide. All levels are subject to change.

FACT & FICTION

This series provides early fluent readers the opportunity to develop reading comprehension strategies and increase fluency. These books are appropriate for guided, shared, and independent reading.

FACT The left-hand pages incorporate realistic photographs to enhance readers' understanding of informational text.

FICTION The right-hand pages engage readers with an entertaining, narrative story that is supported by whimsical illustrations.

The Fact and Fiction pages can be read separately to improve comprehension through questioning, predicting, making inferences, and summarizing. They can also be read side-by-side, in spreads, which encourages students to explore and examine different writing styles.

FACT OR FICTION? This fun quiz helps reinforce students' understanding of what is real and not real.

SPEED READ The text-only version of each section includes word-count rulers for fluency practice and assessment.

GLOSSARY Higher-level vocabulary and concepts are defined in the glossary.

SandCastle™ would like to hear from you.

Tell us your stories about reading this book. What was your favorite page? Was there something hard that you needed help with? Share the ups and downs of learning to read. To get posted on the ABDO Publishing Company Web site, send us an e-mail at:

sandcastle@abdopublishing.com

Roosters crow not only at dawn but at any time of day. Crowing is one way roosters define their territory.

It's 6:00 a.m., and Rex Rooster's alarm clock goes off. He hits the snooze button and thinks to himself, "Just 10 more minutes. Then I'll get up and crow."

If a rooster is not present in a flock of chickens, a hen might stop laying eggs and begin to crow.

It's 6:10 a.m., and Rex's alarm clock goes off again. He says to his wife, Helen Hen, "Honey, would you take over the crowing duties, please? I'm not lazy, but I'm just not a morning chicken."

7

Chickens are daytime animals. At night
they are inactive and roost close together
on a perch.

FLY-INS WELCOME

Rex thinks about different jobs and decides to open a beauty salon. "I'm my own boss now," he says happily. "I don't have to go to work until noon if I don't want to!"

BARBER BARN

REX

YODEL

FLYING GEESE BALLET

BARBER BARN

COMB 'N' CURL

9

Both hens and roosters have combs on the tops of their heads. However, roosters' combs are larger.

Rex specializes in comb styling. He hangs a poster on the wall so that his customers can see what styles are available.

Chickens peck each other to figure out their rank. That's where the phrase *pecking order* comes from. Chickens higher in the order have better access to food and nesting locations.

During his first day of business, Rex takes his family and friends ahead of everyone else. Grandpa Ralph Rooster sits in the first chair and says, "Rex, I'm no spring chicken, and I don't need a fancy comb-over. Just give me the single."

Hens breathe almost twice as fast as roosters.

Rex's next customer is Helen. She is breathless with excitement. She asks, "Rex, do you think the buttercup would look good on me?"

Rex clucks, "Honey, everything looks good on you!"

Chickens' combs are a showy body part, but they also help chickens stay cool.

Helen has also brought their son Chip Chick for his first comb-out. Rex says to Chip, "Son, I think either the walnut or the strawberry would be a cool style for you. Which one would you like?"

"Oh, Dad! Give me the walnut, please!" Chip exclaims.

17

There are about 175 varieties of chickens, which are grouped into about 60 breeds.

By the end of the first week,
Rex has styled the combs of 60
chickens. He locks the door and
says to himself, "I'm exhausted!
Maybe crowing at dawn wasn't
such a bad job after all!"

FACT or Fiction?

Read each statement below. Then decide whether it's from the FACT section or the Fiction section!

1. Crowing is one way roosters define their territory.

2. Chickens use alarm clocks to wake up on time.

3. Chickens go to beauty salons to have their combs styled.

4. Chickens peck each other to figure out their rank.

ANSWERS
1. fact 2. fiction 3. fiction 4. fact

Roosters crow not only at dawn but at any time of   11
day. Crowing is one way roosters define their territory.   20

If a rooster is not present in a flock of chickens, a   32
hen might stop laying eggs and begin to crow.   41

Chickens are daytime animals. At night they are   49
inactive and roost close together on a perch.   57

Both hens and roosters have combs on the tops of   67
their heads. However, roosters' combs are larger.   74

Chickens peck each other to figure out their rank.   83
That's where the phrase pecking order comes from.   91
Chickens higher in the order have better access to   100
food and nesting locations.   104

Hens breathe almost twice as fast as roosters.   112

Chickens' combs are a showy body part, but they   121
also help chickens stay cool.   126

There are about 175 varieties of chickens, which are   135
grouped into about 60 breeds.   140

It's 6:00 a.m., and Rex Rooster's alarm clock goes off. He hits the snooze button and thinks to himself, "Just 10 more minutes. Then I'll get up and crow."

It's 6:10 a.m., and Rex's alarm clock goes off again. He says to his wife, Helen Hen, "Honey, would you take over the crowing duties, please? I'm not lazy, but I'm just not a morning chicken."

Rex thinks about different jobs and decides to open a beauty salon. "I'm my own boss now," he says happily. "I don't have to go to work until noon if I don't want to!"

Rex specializes in comb styling. He hangs a poster on the wall so that his customers can see what styles are available.

During his first day of business, Rex takes his family and friends ahead of everyone else. Grandpa Ralph Rooster sits in the first chair and says, "Rex, I'm no spring chicken, and I don't need a fancy comb-over. Just give me the single."

Rex's next customer is Helen. She is breathless with excitement. She asks, "Rex, do you think the buttercup would look good on me?"

Rex clucks, "Honey, everything looks good on you!"

Helen has also brought their son Chip Chick for his first comb-out. Rex says to Chip, "Son, I think either the walnut or the strawberry would be a cool style for you. Which one would you like?"

"Oh, Dad! Give me the walnut, please!" Chip exclaims.

By the end of the first week, Rex has styled the combs of 60 chickens. He locks the door and says to himself, "I'm exhausted! Maybe crowing at dawn wasn't such a bad job after all!"

GLOSSARY

access. the right to use something, enter a place, or talk to someone

comb. the fleshy crest on the head of a bird

crow. to make the loud, shrill cry of a rooster

flock. a group of animals or birds that have gathered or been herded together

hen. an adult female chicken

rank. one's social class or position in a group

roost. to sit or sleep on a perch

rooster. an adult male chicken

spring chicken. 1) a young chicken 2) a slang expression meaning *young person*

To see a complete list of SandCastle™ books and other nonfiction titles from ABDO Publishing Company, visit www.abdopublishing.com or contact us at: 4940 Viking Drive, Edina, Minnesota 55435 • 1-800-800-1312 • fax: 1-952-831-1632